DANGEROUS JOBS™

ASTRONAUTS
IN ACTION

Lissette Gonzalez

PowerKiDS press.

Published in 2008 by The Rosen Publishing Group, Inc.
29 East 21st Street, New York, NY 10010

First Edition

Editor: Jennifer Way
Book Design: Greg Tucker
Photo Researcher: Nicole Pristash

Photo Credits: Cover, pp. 5, 9, 11, 13, 15, 19 © NASA; p. 7 © Capt. Michael Cumberworth/U.S. Air Force; p. 17 © NASA-DFRC; p. 21 © NASA/Kim Shiflett.

Library of Congress Cataloging-in-Publication Data

Gonzalez, Lissette, 1968–
    Astronauts in action / Lissette Gonzalez.
        p. cm. — (Dangerous jobs)
    Includes bibliographical references and index.
    ISBN-13: 978-1-4042-3776-6 (library binding)
    ISBN-10: 1-4042-3776-3 (library binding)
    1. Astronautics—Juvenile literature. 2. Astronauts—Juvenile literature. I. Title.
    TL793.G635 2008
    629.45—dc22
                                            2006037472

Manufactured in the United States of America

CONTENTS

ASTRONAUTS

Astronauts have dangerous jobs. They travel into outer space in **space shuttles**. In the United States, astronauts work for the National Aeronautics and Space Administration, or NASA.

In space people need special supplies and training to stay safe. At NASA's training school, astronauts learn how to work a spacecraft safely. For two years they prepare for their trip, from liftoff to return.

Even though it is a dangerous job, many people try to see if they have what it takes to become an astronaut. Each year only about 100 people are chosen to go to astronaut school.

Although it is a dangerous job, many people hope to become an astronaut. This astronaut is floating outside a shuttle in outer space.

BEFORE THEY WERE ASTRONAUTS

When the space **program** began in 1959, the first astronauts were people who had served in the military. Today any American may apply to NASA's astronaut training program. However, to be considered, a person must have studied many different fields of science.

Before they are chosen for the program, astronauts must pass tests to prove they are healthy enough to work in space. They must also show that they are good team players who can work well with the other astronauts and the ground crew.

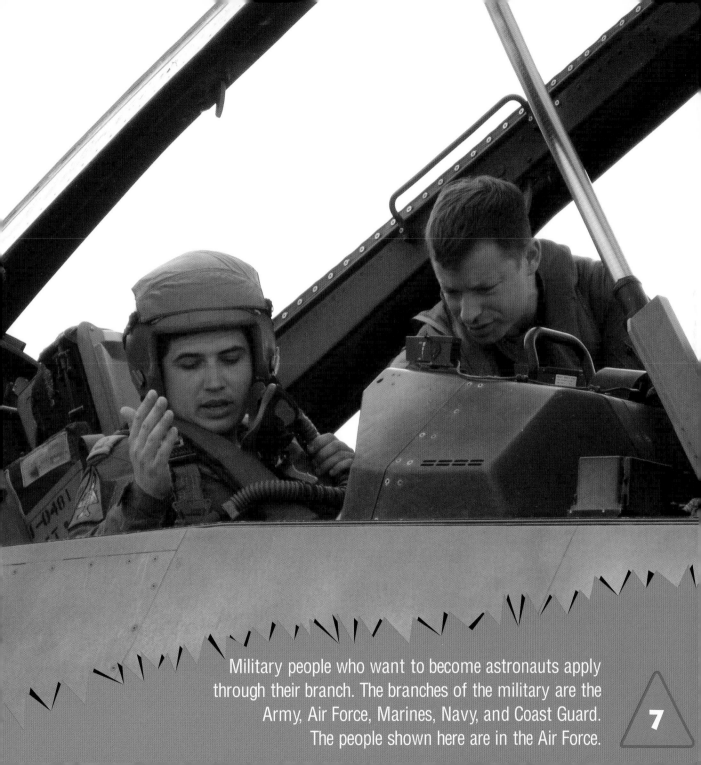

Military people who want to become astronauts apply through their branch. The branches of the military are the Army, Air Force, Marines, Navy, and Coast Guard. The people shown here are in the Air Force.

7

ASTRONAUT TRAINING

Astronauts undergo a year of basic training at NASA's Johnson Space Center, near Houston, Texas. At the center, astronauts learn how to operate the space shuttle and take classes in rocket science.

Astronauts also practice wearing their **protective** space suits. These heavy suits help keep them safe from the **radiation**, cold, and heat of space.

To get the astronauts used to the feeling of being in space, NASA puts them on weightless training flights. The KC-135 airplanes fly up and then dive toward the ground. As a plane falls, everything inside it floats up, just as it would in space!

The astronauts sometimes call the KC-135 the Vomit Comet because the exercises can make them sick to their stomachs.

9

BLAST OFF!

NASA's astronauts spend hundreds of hours working with supplies and computer programs that look and act just like spacecraft. Everyone practices the steps of the **mission**, from liftoff to touchdown, and learns to prepare for an **emergency**.

Liftoff is the most dangerous time in a mission. It can be the scariest few minutes of an astronaut's life. Inside the shuttle the force of the liftoff makes the astronauts feel as if something heavy was pressing down on their bodies. This makes it hard to breathe. Some astronauts say that this feels like an elephant is sitting on your chest!

This is a space shuttle blasting off. There are many possible dangers during liftoff. It takes a lot of people with special skills to make a liftoff go smoothly.

11

DANGERS IN SPACE

When the shuttle reaches its top speed, the astronauts will be flying at almost 18,000 miles per hour (28,968 km/h). While in **orbit** they feel as if they are weightless. Most astronauts get used to feeling weightless and quickly begin to go about their work.

One of the most dangerous things about working in space is radiation. Too much radiation can make you sick. The **atmosphere** on Earth protects people, animals, and plants from radiation. Whenever astronauts travel outside this atmosphere, their bodies get more radiation than they would on Earth.

Astronauts wear special space suits when they are outside the shuttle in space. These suits protect their bodies from amounts of radiation that could make them sick.

13

SPACE ACCIDENTS

Most of NASA's space missions have been carried out safely. There have been accidents, or unexpected and bad events, though. The first U.S. astronauts to die in flight were the crew of the *Challenger* in 1986. One of these astronauts was Christa McAuliffe, the first teacher in space. *Challenger* exploded, or blew up.

In 2003, the space shuttle *Columbia* and its crew of seven were killed as they returned to Earth. Some of the tiles that protect *Columbia* from heat and cold had broken. This caused the shuttle to crash. To date 17 U.S. astronauts have died on the job.

14

The *Challenger* exploded because of a broken seal that let fire escape from the booster rockets. The seven astronauts on board died 73 seconds after liftoff.

15

RETURNING TO EARTH

Most U.S. astronauts' missions last about a week. Astronauts who work on the **International Space Station**, however, can stay in space for up to three months.

The return to Earth is the second-most-dangerous part of being an astronaut. Astronauts must be careful to prepare their bodies for the return. Their bodies lose a lot of water while in space. Drinking plenty of water helps lessen the chances that they will black out during reentry. This is most important for the pilot, who is in charge of operating the shuttle.

The return to Earth is a kind of fall that is controlled by the pilot. The parachute on the back of this landing space shuttle helps it slow down safely.

17

HELP FROM BELOW

The ground crew is the group of people at the space center who help the astronauts. While in space, astronauts stay in touch with the NASA ground crew's flight controllers. Flight controllers help look after the shuttle, but the safety of the astronauts is their main duty. This makes the flight controller's job very important.

Sometimes the ground crew has only seconds to make important decisions. In 1985, flight controller Jenny Howard Stein was in charge when the space shuttle had engine trouble. Within seconds Stein decided that it was safe to go on. This saved the astronauts from danger.

The ground crew works outside and around the space shuttle to make sure that all the parts of the shuttle are working the way they should.

19

AFTER THE MISSION ENDS

After they land, astronauts must get used to being on Earth. Most astronauts will lose **muscle** while they are in space. Without **gravity** they are weightless. Their muscles have no force to work against and become weakened. The longer an astronaut stays in space, the worse this problem will be. Some astronauts even report muscle pains that last for months after their missions.

NASA looks after the health of astronauts over the long term. So far it appears that astronauts seem to get back to good health and live as long as people who have never been in space.

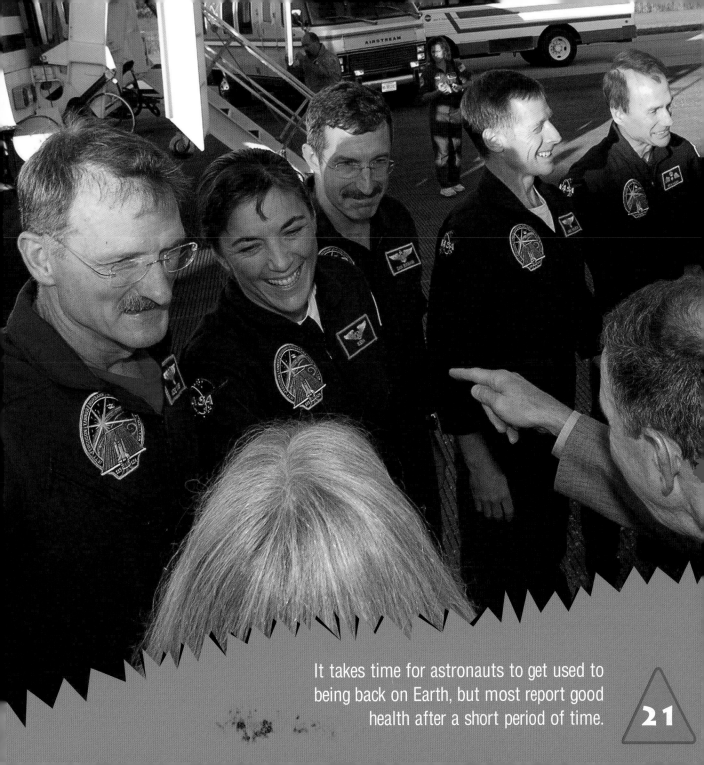

It takes time for astronauts to get used to being back on Earth, but most report good health after a short period of time.

21

SCIENCE AND SERVICE

Astronauts say that flying in space is a once in a lifetime **experience**. Even though their jobs are dangerous, they love what they do. They experience things other people do not. For example, they get to see the beautiful Earth from space.

Astronauts know that the work they do will help not only their country but also people all over the world. On some shuttle missions, American astronauts have worked with Russian astronauts on the International Space Station. The science experiments these astronauts do in space might one day help produce new inventions that people can use on Earth.

GLOSSARY

atmosphere (AT-muh-sfeer) The gases around an object in space.

emergency (ih-MUR-jin-see) An event that happens in which quick help is needed.

experience (ik-SPEER-ee-ents) Knowledge or skill gained by doing or seeing something.

gravity (GRA-vih-tee) The natural force that causes objects to move toward the center of Earth.

International Space Station (in-ter-NA-shuh-nul SPAYS STAY-shun) A very large building in space where astronauts from all over the world go to study space. It should be finished in 2010.

mission (MIH-shun) A special job or task.

muscle (MUH-sul) A part of the body that makes the body move.

orbit (OR-bit) A circular path.

program (PROH-gram) Something that is done by a group for a purpose.

protective (pruh-TEKT-iv) Having to do with keeping things safe.

radiation (ray-dee-AY-shun) Rays of light, heat, or power that spread outward from something. The Sun's light is radiation.

space shuttles (SPAYS SHUH-tulz) Spacecraft made to carry people and goods to and from space.

INDEX

WEB SITES

Due to the changing nature of Internet links, PowerKids Press has developed an online list of Web sites related to the subject of this book. This site is updated regularly. Please use this link to access the list:

www.powerkidslinks.com/djob/astronaut/